DEMAIN PUBLISHING

<u>Short Sharp Shocks!</u>

Book 0: Dirty Paws - Dean M. Drinkel
Book 1: Patient K - Barbie Wilde
Book 2: The Stranger & The Ribbon – Tim Dry
Book 3: Asylum Of Shadows – Stephanie Ellis
Book 4: Monster Beach – Ritchie Valentine Smith
Book 5: Beasties & Other Stories – Martin Richmond
Book 6: Every Moon Atrocious – Emile-Louis Tomas Jouvet
Book 7: A Monster Met – Liz Tuckwell
Book 8: The Intruders & Other Stories – Jason D. Brawn
Book 9: The Other – David Youngquist
Book 10: Symphony Of Blood – Leah Crowley
Book 11: Shattered – Anthony Watson
Book 12: The Devil's Portion – Benedict J. Jones
Book 13: Cinders Of A Blind Man Who Could See – Kev Harrison
Book 14: Dulce Et Decorum Est – Dan Howarth
Book 15: Blood, Bears & Dolls – Allison Weir
Book 16: The Forest Is Hungry – Chris Stanley
Book 17: The Town That Feared Dusk – Calvin Demmer
Book 18: Night Of The Rider – Alyson Faye
Book 19: Isidora's Pawn – Erik Hofstatter
Book 20: Plain – D.T. Griffith
Book 21: Supermassive Black Mass – Matthew Davis

Book 46: The Birthday Girl & Other Stories –
        Christopher Beck
Book 47: Crowded House & Other Stories - S.J.
        Budd
Book 48: Hand To Mouth – Deborah Sheldon
Book 49: Moonlight Gunshot Mallet Flame / A
        Little Death – Alicia Hilton
Book 50: Dark Corners - David Charlesworth

Murder! Mystery! Mayhem!

Maggie Of My Heart – Alyson Faye
The Funeral Birds – Paula R.C. Readman
Cursed – Paul M. Feeney
The Bone Factory – Yolanda Sfetsos
Garland Cove – Deborah Sheldon
Death In The Dugout – Bruce Harris

Beats! Ballads! Blank Verse!

Book 1: Echoes From An Expired Earth – Allen
Ashley
Book 2: Grave Goods – Cardinal Cox
Book 3: From Long Ago – Paul Woodward
Book 4: Laws Of Discord – William Clunie
Book 5: Fanged Dandelion – Eric LaRocca
Book 6: Halloween's Best Cellar – Martin
Richmond
Book 7: Existential Jibber Jabber – Marc Shapiro

Weird! Wonderful! Other Worlds

Book 1: The Raven King – Liz Tuckwell
Book 2: The Wired City – Yolanda Sfetsos

Horror Novels & Novellas

House Of Wrax – Raven Dane
And Blood Did Fall – Chad A. Clark
The Fallen – Anthony Watson
The Underclass – Dan Weatherer
Cheslyn Myre – Dan Weatherer
Greenbeard – John Travis
Tower Of Raven – Kevin M. Folliard
Welcome Home Natalie – Reyna Young
Little Bird – TR Hitchman
Society Place – Andrew David Barker
Axe – Terry Grimwood
Wicked Blood – E.C. Hanson
Between The Teeth Of Charon – Grant Longstaff
The Again-Walkers – Deborah Sheldon

Science Fiction Novels & Novellas

Odyssey Of The Black Turtle – Paul Woodward
Sons Of Sol – Kevin R. McNally

The 'A QUIET APOCALYPSE' Series

A Quiet Apocalypse – Dave Jeffery
Cathedral (A Quiet Apocalypse Book 2) – Dave Jeffery
The Samaritan (A Quiet Apocalypse Book 3) – Dave Jeffery
A Silent Dystopia (Stories Of A Quiet Apocalypse) – Edited by D.T. Griffith

Tribunal (A Quiet Apocalypse Book 4) – Dave Jeffery

General Fiction

Joe – Terry Grimwood
Finding Jericho – Dave Jeffery

Science Fiction Collections

Vistas – Chris Kelso

Horror Fiction Collections

Distant Frequencies – Frank Duffy
Where We Live – Tim Cooke
Night Voices – Paul Edwards & Frank Duffy

Anthologies

The Darkest Battlefield – Tales Of WW1/Horror

HALLOWEEN'S BEST CELLAR

POEMS BY
MARTIN RICHMOND

A BEATS! BALLADS! BLANK VERSE! BOOK

BOOK 6

CONTENTS

A treasury of fun, spooky tales told in rhyme.
Stuffing chills and chuckles into, 'Once upon a time'.

For Spooky Sheila

INTRODUCTION

Halloween time is here, so where should you go for a thoroughly chilly experience? Inside the fridge? No? Not that kind of a chill you're after? Well put down the ice lolly and go visit the scariest room in the house, which, of course, has to be the cellar, that's if you're unlucky enough to have one?

You do realise that it's located underground, so you're on a level with coffins and worms and dead people in graveyards, which can't be good, can it? But then, with all the spooks and monsters stomping and slithering around in the dark down there, you must ask yourself, do you feel brave enough to join them? Of course you do, so go on, put on your mask and get down there, what have you got to lose? Well, I can think of a few things, but do it anyway, and mind that first step—it isn't there!

Halloween's Best Cellar is *the* place to go to join the world of ghoulies, ghosties, long-leggedy beasties and things that go BOO in the night. These rhyme tale adventures guide you through a trapdoor, down a flight of cellar steps in the darkest darkness, allowing you to carry only a flickering candle with you into the deepest corners of HALLOWEEN.

Ignore the blood curdling yells as you descend the rickety wooden staircase, you'll soon be sick of screaming like that. Pause to brush away all the cobwebs that suddenly cling to your face, when a hundred, tiny, scampering legs swarm madly across your skin, seeking somewhere warm to hide. You never know, some of them might even be harmless? But you'll soon shake most of them off and maybe even shoo away some of your darkest fears to continue down, deeper into the icy blackness.

The staircase is quite steep, creaking loudly with every step you make and the light from the open trapdoor above you becomes fainter and fainter as you travel deeper and deeper—and deeper. Just how deep can this cellar be?

You hear a scurrying, scratching noise below you, beyond the glow of the candle, almost hiding the faint chatter of many, distant voices—almost.

But curiosity keeps you going down, even though your fear is increasing and scraping away at your heart, urging you not to look behind you, even though you do. But then, drops of liquid splash down into your eye, and as you wipe them away you wonder, since you can't see it, is it really dripping water—or blood? You're almost there now, the handrail has got a slimy feel to it and the smell of something rotten is growing stronger. Maybe you shouldn't have had that extra chocolate-chip muffin after all as it may soon get very messy?

Suddenly, the trapdoor above you slams shut with an almighty "BANG" and the draft from it blows out the candle's flame! Shaking, in a cold sweat, you feel someone with extremely cold fingers grip onto your hand and pull it away from the rail. You try to cry out, but an icy finger touches your lips, urging you to silence as you're guided slowly down to the foot of the stair. The helping hand, with more than the usual five fingers, vanishes!

Strange voices echo across the cellar, telling tales told in rhyme. You can hear an audience is shuffling about, gathering around you, many faceless creatures from many impossible worlds who are also very keen to hear the strangest of tales about themselves. But they don't like interruptions, not even from slightly noisy breathing, so hold your breath, here we go...

Martin Richmond – September 2021

MYTHS & LEGENDS

THE PIRATE'S GRISLY TALE

T'was on a filthy night such as this,
when the thunder gave the clouds a kiss
and lightning branched the heavens wide
to silver the tears it could not hide.

As the moon fought the clouds to glimpse
a murderous scene to force it to wince
and wish that it had never really tried
to see how it was that the pirate died?

Captain Kraken made a pact with Hell,
a devil with a devil's soul to sell,
and crewed his sailing ship 'The Iron
Demon'
with thirteen skeletons instead of
seamen.

He plundered the oceans turning them
red
taking treasure and pleasure, leaving
dead,
the crews and passengers of cargo ships
tearing off their very flesh in strips.

Man, woman and child, showing mercy
for none,
shredding souls for the devil to feed
upon.
Taking their ships, their gold and silver
too
they ruled the waves as pirates often do.

The tyrant, Kraken, drove his crew with
fear
to massacre night and day for o'er a
year.
Toiling endlessly, scrubbing bloody decks
of an abattoir afloat in a Sargasso of
wrecks.

But a mutiny now showed it's hand
from the thirteen pirates of his bony band
who rebelled against the Captain's view
that rest was not for a skeleton crew.

Seizing their Captain they carried him
high
up the gusting rigging ignoring his cry
of, "Unhand me, blackguards, let me go,"
they impaled him above the nest of the
crow.

Pierced upon the masthead, still barely
alive,
a lightning bolt struck, splitting him wide.
and blasting his motley, rebellious crew
to the four winds as they furiously blew.

The ship sailed on and I'm told is sailing
still,
as a ghost, 'The Iron Demon', with an icy
chill
reminder to pirates who hire devils to
shout it,
"GOOD CREWS ARE HARD TO COME BY,
 MAKE NO BONES ABOUT IT!"

RIDDLE OF THE MUMMY

Rameses the third, an Egyptian
pharaoh
of three thousand years ago,
awoke with a splitting headache
and a desperate need to go.

He frantically needed the
bathroom,
he was busting to go very soon,
so pushing off the lid of his
sarcophagus
he glanced round the walls of his
tomb.

He recalled taking a sleeping
draught
and going straight off to his bed.
They shook him when he failed to
wake up
so mistakenly presumed he was
dead!

Thinking he must have passed
away

he was mummified and placed in
a tomb.
He awoke in a darkened museum,
but thought he was still in his
room.

The full moon shone through the
skylight
lighting up King Rameses the
third,
who stumbled across the marble
floor
quite unable to utter a single
word.

Rameses peeked through a
doorway,
he still needed to get some relief.
Clutching dangling bandages he
strutted,
tensely clenching his crumbling
teeth.

He came to the top of an unlit
staircase
spiralling away down three floors.

His wrappings tangled and down
he tumbled
screaming out with muffled roars.

He hurtled down the stairway,
cartwheeling,
bouncing from the banister to the
wall.
He came to rest with a resounding
CRASH,
at the foot of the stair, in the hall.

The curator found him next
morning
his yellowed bandages all in a
muddle.
As dead as an ancient Egyptian
should be,
and seated in a great big puddle!

THE LEGACY OF KING MIDAS

The golden medallion of King Midas
was lifted from sand beneath his tomb.
The native digger, Don, who found it
turned golden yellow in the gloom.

His pal, an experienced digger,
just about as greedy as the first.
Solidified their long friendship,
in a quite sudden, glittering burst.

Within two days the entire crew
of the excavation team were gold.
Except Sir Simon Truscot-Potts
who was stuck in bed with a cold.

When word spread about the medallion
the Egyptian army moved right in.
They now have two, shiny, yellow tanks,
gold soldiers and a war they can't win.

Sir Simon soon left his sick bed
to survey all the 24 carat crowd.
"Hordes of golden people," he thought,

"Is melting down humans allowed?"

He had the gold removed and sold
and had a huge grand palace built.
He bought everything he'd ever wanted
without feeling any lingering gilt!

He didn't need to lift the medallion
he left it there, right where it lay.
And if he needed some extra cash
he would send a butler with a tray.

Butlers, he found, were plentiful,
Their help was quite easy to find,
all now worth their weight in gold,
especially the most trusting kind.

They say money doesn't buy happiness,
his wife Goldie would probably agree.
And if she could talk she would tell you,
but then silence is golden you see!

GORGON STYLE

Onto the threshold the lady glided,
in from the dark, rain-swept street.
The hooded cloak hid the features
of a person you wouldn't like to meet.

Miss Carol Ann, the hairdresser,
preoccupied, gestured to a chair.
The lady sat and threw off her hood
revealing her most fearsome glare.

Kelly looked up from a magazine
and turned a darker shade of grey.
Jacqueline glanced from her hairdryer,
her complexion now resembling clay.

Miss Carol Ann, without turning round,
waved her young assistant across.
"Finish this lady off now, Emma?"
you could tell that she was the boss.

Mrs Medusa glided eerily forward
when Carol Ann called out, "Next!"
She seated herself at the mirror,
Miss Carol Ann looked perplexed.

Gazing at the writhing, hissing scalp,
Miss Carol Ann scratched her ear.
"You're in the wrong place, Madam,
the pet shop's next door, my dear!"

THE HEADLESS HORSEMAN COMETH

Beware to the lonely traveller,
walking in New England's woods,
a terrifying sight will gallop by,
chilling the warmest of bloods.

On a fiery, wild, black steed
the headless horseman appears,
without any warning he charges,
his sword swinging as he nears.

It will sever your foolish head,
clean from off your shoulder,
no worries of getting grey hair,
you won't be getting any older.

The swish of blood-soaked blade,
the demon hoof beats closing in,
you toss a coin to escape death,
heads you lose, beneath the chin.

The horrific, headless horseman,
once rode this trail, a poor stranger,
he ignored the signs beside the road,

CAREFUL, LOW BRANCHES, DANGER!

KEEP AN EYE OUT FOR THE CYCLOPS

The explorer discovered the Cyclops' lair
hidden not so far away from man.
Trapped in a cage he vented his rage
at the explorer's masterful plan.

"How did you find me?" he bellowed,
his single orb blinking at the sky.
"It was easy," said the explorer,
"it's in the phonebook, under I."

"I should have gone without a phone,"
said the Cyclops, with dejection.
"I also got you by your optician,
your eyeglass is ready for
collection."

"Other tell-tale hints and tiny clues
led me to your door today."
"Like putting, C.Y. CLOPS,"
on your letterbox,
was a bit of a dead give-away."

"What happens now?" Cyclops wailed.

"I don't want to be locked in a zoo."
"Don't worry Cy, "said the explorer,
"I've a job as a private eye for you."

THE TRUE STORY OF JACK AND THE BEANSTALK

Soon after Jack had planted his beans,
not Heinz, but magic, you know what that means.
A giant plant sprouted, pushing up to the sky,
everyone could see it towering on high.

Jack nipped into a local market
for a carton of goat's milk for his Mum.
Since he'd sold the cow for a few beans
he was rubbing a rear that was numb.

Gazing up he swore it was closer
than the huge plant had been before,
watching it come nearer and nearer
to the car park of the store next door!

Fearful, he ran Westwards, it followed,
running off to the South, it came too.
Hour upon hour it constantly chased,
and still higher the plant thing grew!

He collapsed on a park bench exhausted,

several miles away from his home.
"Those awful magic beans," he wailed,
"why won't this vine *leaf* me alone"?
Each day it's shadow covered him,
blotting out the sun as he walked.
If only poor Jack had known the truth
and realise that he'd been stalked!

JACK

YE OLDE SNICKET MONSTER

In the historical English city of York,
where Vikings lived and Romans walked,
exists many a dark and narrow alley
in which you really shouldn't dally.

The alleys, or Snickets as locals say,
between buildings, avoid the light of day.
Due to its slender width, so very narrow,
walking singly deeply chills the marrow.

Somewhere between its start and end,
some go missing; you may lose a friend.
Snatched in the Snicket monster's grip
none ever lives to recount their trip.

Whisked right away to who knows where,
leaving not a single trace to its lair.
Its voracious appetite knows no bounds,
its gnashing teeth are echoing sounds.

No blood stains, just scratches on wall,
shows that the creature exists at all.
Those who've vanished into thin air,
never screamed as its talons tear.

We know it exists and where it lurks,
in Snicket shadows it silently works.
Taking the stragglers in mid-breath,
introducing them to a mystery death.

The Vikings knew it, the Romans too,
the Victorians tried catching it
but we haven't got a clue,
where it came from or where it hides,
but Yorkies avoid the Snicket's sides.

The tourists in their thousands flock,
providing it snacks around the clock.
So avoid the alleyways, if you can,
to halt the monster's master plan.

To tear and rip, spindle and mutilate,
to eradicate all trace and seal your fate.
Visit York, wallow in its historic past
but avoid Snickets or the visit will be...
...your last!

DRAGONMEAT

Drinkel the butcher had a roaring trade,
his customers queued around the clock.
A short while ago he couldn't sell
anything,
no blood had stained his butcher's block.

Ever since he began selling Dragonmeat
his fortunes are really on the mend.
His succulent barbecued steaks,
are sending people round the bend.

A dark-suited gent with a briefcase
poked his nose into the shop.
"You can't do it Mr Drinkel," he said,
"keep it up and I'll call a cop!"

"Why, what's wrong, what have I done,
tell me, where's the imagined crime?"
Mr Drinkel suddenly stopped in mid chop,
of a rib that was dragon-ishly prime.

"You're selling meat described as Dragon,
when there's really no such thing."
The Health department gent squeaked

as though he was about to sing.

"It *is* Dragon meat and I can prove it,
just slither round the counter, follow me."
Mr Drinkel trotted out to the back yard
carrying a large, antique, cellar key.

Down dark cellar steps they trooped,
Mr Drinkel was leading the way.
The Health man was close on his heels
not really knowing what to say?

They finally reached the cellar floor
walking down a passage, dimly lit.
They came to a door at the end
and Mr Drinkel said, "Well, this is it!"

He opened the creaking oak door
and switched on a solitary light.
There, sat in the corner, was a dragon,
yes, a real, live dragon, that's right.

The man couldn't believe his eyes,
a creature, scaly green, was snoozing.
"Well," said Mr Drinkel, "are you happy,
now that I've proved what we're using?"

"Hold on," said the man in the suit,
carefully putting his briefcase down.
"How can you be selling Dragon meat,
when there's only *one* to be found?"

"Oh yes," said Mr Drinkel strolling over
and tapped the dragon sharply on the
tail.
The dragon leapt up belching flames,
turning the Health man dark red from
pale.

The suit was burned right off him
and his body was charcoal roasted.
Mr Drinkel produced a meat cleaver
and then very loudly he boasted.

"I didn't say it was *made* from dragons
only that it was prime, *dragon meat*!"
"You're the fifth Health man we've had
and you're all going down a treat!"

THE SWEET TOOTH FAIRY

Does anyone know what happens
when the Tooth Fairy's tooth falls out?
Is there a back-up squad
from the land of nod,
just what are these fairies all about?

Do fairies have teeth and if so,
is there a fairy dental scheme?
Are there little pillows
for the flighty fellows,
to hide a loose molar in a dream?

Do they get a gold or silver coin
left for the tooth that has decayed?
Do they even floss
to prevent the loss,
where is fairy toothpaste made?

If they eat nothing but fairy cakes
their teeth would never harden.
All fairies would be fat,
can you imagine that,
bulging from the bottom of your garden!

Fairy dentists don't use smelly gas
or sharp needles that might sting.
Make an appointment now,
they'll show you exactly how,
go on, give the dentist a fairy ring!

When you wake up late one night
and you find your tooth has gone!
The fairy must have been
it wasn't just a dream,
'cos they pick up ev-fairy-one!

If you live way across the water
and of dentists you're quite wary.
Don't you sob and fret,
be sure your Mum'll get,
a call to the Cross Channel fairy!

THE CAMPAIGN AGAINST SANTA CLAUS

In dead of night a fat, bearded fellow
slips very quietly inside your home.
Carries a sack, wears a blood-red suit,
And you allow this psycho to roam?

He leaves presents for your children
but never leaves one for you.
He comes and goes as he pleases,
why you let him I haven't a clue?

He doesn't enter by the front door,
he's just entirely lost the plot.
His bulk squeezes down the chimney
whether you've got one or not!

Hooded, he skulks in the dark
downing mince pies and milk.
For all you know his underwear
could be black, frilly and silk?

The snow piles up on the ground
and he lands right up on the roof.
Whipping reindeers till their noses glow,

well, do you need more proof?

Don't trust this flying tub of lard,
don't let this red monster inside.
Why doesn't he let himself be seen,
what on earth has he got to hide?

Is it a coincidence he rides a *sleigh,*
the misspelling of a serial killer?
Gaining your confidence he'll attack,
he's not even a good stocking filler.

Don't forget he's got your lists
and he's checked them twice.
Really he's seeking out the naughty,
he's not interested in the nice.

He's a father without any kids,
drives free transport through the snows.
He only works one day of the year,
I wonder if the taxman knows?

Join the campaign and ban Santa now.
Stop him committing his criminal act.
Don't let him get his clause in you,
come on, let's get this toy boy sacked!

NOT QUITE YETI

The mountain climbers halted
in their quest to reach the top,
of one of the bleak Himalayas,
a cold, inhospitable spot.

Two of the brave men stood,
consulting an ancient map,
the third removed his backpack
and began to loosen the strap.

He sat midst the blanket of snow,
the frost fringed his beard with white,
his breath blew mist cross his vision,
through gloves he felt the frost bite.

Before his eyes stepped a huge figure
more than a hundred yards away,
its height was eight feet, maybe more,
covered in a shaggy coat of grey.

Through its fur glinted two steely eyes,
its bear-like feet crunched the snow,
as it moved away down the slope,
the climber, dumb-struck, watched it go.

"It's the – the," stuttered the climber,
pointing at the thing shuffling away.
"the ablobol – abomol - ablomm,"
the word he could not say.

The creature turned in his direction
its eyes burning like hot coal.
The monster staggered toward him,
he felt a terror penetrate his soul.

It leaned in close and whispered,
"Finding you was fantastic luck,
I've been wandering about for hours,
the zip on my onesie's stuck!"

MONSTERS & DEVILS

THE FEATURES OF SWAMP CREATURES

Deep in the Everglades heavy mist
swirled,
a flock of birds, startled, broke the air.
Bursting from the swamp two figures
arose,
Mud-green slime dripping from their
hair.

They both moved in perfect harmony,
ploughing chest-high through the
water,
matching each other's reflective
motion,
the silver moon offering a last quarter.

Their gargoyle-like heads submerged,
their reptilian feet sliced through the
air,
their mirror-image moves continued
on,
no chilling display could ever compare.

Both creatures pleased beyond
measure,
with slime-oozing mouths sickly
grinning,
they knew they could win the gold
medal,
for Swampland Synchronised
Swimming.

FRANKENSTEIN'S MONSTER?

"IT'S ALIVE, IT'S ALIVE," he cried,
illuminated by flashing blue sparks.
High voltage burst through its body,
leaving jagged scars and birth marks.

Steel bolts protruded from its neck
and from its tiny, exposed brain,
oozed a green, bubbling mess
from where it had long since lain.

Piece by piece, so carefully made,
with the most tender, loving care,
stitching each finger, toe and nostril
and gluing on every single hair.

Seven foot six in its stocking feet
the evident pride of its creator.
Taking itself to life's tragic stage
with a Gothic castle as its theatre.

It can't communicate with fellow man,
it just grunts and snorts and mumbles.
Walking awkwardly, like a new-born,

learning gradually as it stumbles.

We all will discover its true vocation,
a history both devious and sinister.
Good intentions always end in misery,
the way of every new Prime Minister.

ALONG CAME A TEN TON SPIDER

Its web was attached to the guttering
below the slate roof of number four,
and across the street to the lamp post,
hung down by the Green's front door.

It had been there since early morning,
well it wasn't there at all last night,
and judging by the cocooned milk van,
I'd say dawn would be about right.

The road-sweeping lorry was unlucky,
coming along today, of all days.
You don't usually see it for ages,
then along it comes - and it stays!

Mrs McLeod from number forty-three,
must have been shocked indeed.
She takes her poodle for walkies early,
now all that's left now is a lead.

Ryan the paper boy delivered his last
and he won't be coming by again.
Read about it if you get your own paper,

or catch it on TV's 'News at Ten.'

The fire brigade couldn't shift the thing,
all that's left is a great deal of water.
Police lost a squad car, three bobbies,
a dog van,
and a long arm that's very much shorter.

Sheila poked a head from the window,
visibly shocked and all of a fluster.
She dashed madly from the house,
wielding a pink feather duster.

The battle was simply amazing,
nothing before or since had been seen,
but in less than it takes to boil a kettle,
the spider and web were wiped clean.

Now the streets are quiet and deserted,
but it won't be staying that way,
the spider she squished was called,
"Junior",
and its Mother is coming to stay!

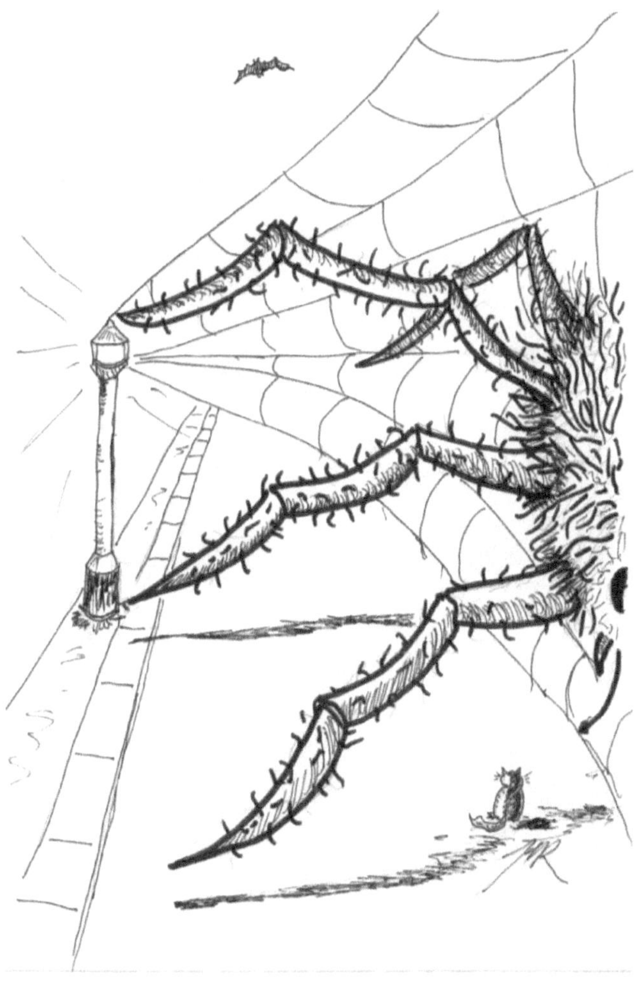

DE – BUGGED

Graeme Buffy dearly loved his work,
he dealt constantly with death you see.
Killing the smallest of God's creatures,
in destroying insects he'd earned a
degree.

He had a small firm called "DE-BUGs"
and white van inscribed with this prayer,
"DE – BUGS are DELETED
AND YOU'LL BE DELIGHTED,
by Mister Buffy, the ant-empire slayer."

A hard hat, goggles and overalls
a backpack ready and rarin' to go,
down to a cellar on a hot, humid day,
a darkness 'neath the wings of a crow.

Graeme descends spreading death
from a cylinder strapped to his back.
A carpet of carapace shells upturn
kicking tiny legs in the poison attack.

Their screams could not be heard,
above the laughter within his mask,

exterminating miniature creatures,
he delighted in his gruesome task.

Job done, sat at the foot of the steps,
his cylinder and mask at his feet,
he blew smoke rings cross the beetles.
"Bugs," he thought, "are easy meat."

Music wafting in through the cellar door
suddenly vanished as the news began.
He recalled the lottery ticket he'd bought,
could he be sitting here a very rich man?

The results were announced and mentally
he marked the numbers off one by one.
"Yes, yes", he repeated excitedly!
"I've won", he shouted, "I'VE WON!

As he waved the ticket about on high
it was snatched from his fingertips.
He turned to see a giant cockroach,
all words instantly froze on his lips.

The cockroach, severed Graeme's head,
explaining, "Each was a close relation,"
this sum will do very nicely I think,
three million pounds in compensation!"

THE BLOB

The awesome slime pulsated,
as it slithered across the floor.
It left a glistening trail behind
as it shuffled through the door.

It headed towards the kitchen,
splodging right through the hall.
A tabby cat arched its back
and scrambled right up the wall.

It squeezed under the kitchen door
and oozed its way right inside.
It slimed up to the kitchen sink,
Mother, washing, almost died.

Screaming a blood-curdling yell
at the thing that drove her mad,
"Get down off there young man,
or I'll go and fetch your Dad."

Mummy blob was extremely angry
with her very naughty little child.
But it only wanted to learn how,
she kept her washday hands so mild?

A DEVIL OF A JOB

The bankrupt face of Donald Hull
was cradled in both his hands.
He'd lost everything he'd owned,
stocks, shares, money, land.

He wept so pitifully over his desk,
a thing he didn't legally possess.
Tears splashed into his whiskey
that he foolishly drank to excess.

He bemoaned his run of bad luck
and all the chances he'd lost,
the dirty deals that'd gone sour
and friends he'd double-crossed.

Definitely not a pleasant man,
devoid of morals or good deeds,
supposing blood was liquid gold,
he'd steal every stone that bleeds.

"I'd sell my soul in a minute,"
he sobbed and cried out loud,
"To be rich once more again
and be better than the crowd."

His office door crashed open,
thick, black smoke poured right in.
Fierce heat singed his eyebrows
and scorched his double chin.

"I'll be burned to a crisp," he cried,
"I - I really don't want to die."
But the smoke vanished instantly
and he wiped a tear from his eye.

Framed in the doorway, a man in black,
black cape, black shirt, and black gloves,
he reminded Mr Hull of a magician,
attempting to conjure up doves.

The man in black removed his hat,
loosening a black scarf at his throat,
Mr Hull was startled to stay the least
at the horns protruding like a goat.

"I am here at your request Mr Hull,"
said the satanic-looking man.
"You offered your soul for sale so,
take a look at my guaranteed plan."

He produced a scroll from his pocket,

all scorched and heavily steaming.
"Sign this now and make your wish,"
his jagged teeth blackly gleaming.

"W - Wish, anything?" he stammered,
trying hard to read the small print.
"Whatever your heart desires friend,"
his oily eyes sparked an evil glint.

"Okay Mr Lucifer, you've got a deal,"
said Mr Hull, scribbling his name.
"A billion pounds right here, right now,
legal, tax free, and won in a game."

"No problem sunshine, there you go."
That's where Mr Hull's life ceases,
as he got the billion pounds as promised,
when he drowned in ten pence pieces.

THE PLANT MAN

The doctor's surgery door burst open,
a man stood screaming in panic.
"DOCTOR, YOU'VE GOT TO HELP ME!"
The doctor jotted down, 'manic!'

"Calm down," soothed the doctor,
"just take it easy now - please."
The man clad in hooded anorak
began to cough and to wheeze.

"How can I help you then, Mister, er?"
A deep hood masked the strange man.
"It's Triffid," he said, removing his coat,
the doctor gasped and nearly ran.

Mr Triffid's head was a tangled bush,
of matted leaves, branches and thorn.
Vines sprang from his ears and nostrils,
over his neck grass grew like a lawn.

Shocked and stunned the doctor spoke
sounding quite frightened at first.
"Good grief, I thought I'd seen it all,
but this...this illness is the worst.".

He composed himself and apologised.
"Sorry old man, it was the shock."
"I do understand," said Mr Triffid,
"please don't worry about it Doc."

"Better get undressed," the doctor said,
not really wanting to see more.
But when Mr Triffid shed his clothing
the doctor fainted to the floor.

Moss-covered fingers glistened with dew
mopped the doctor's fevered cheek,
as the doctor awoke from dreaming,
that he'd performed CPR on a leek!

"Mr Triffid you're a medical marvel,"
said the doctor, sitting back in his chair.
He swatted away the clouds of greenfly
that swarmed from Mr Triffid's hair.

"I don't know what to do Doc," he said,
"it's really quite worrying and queer?"
"I do understand, "said the doctor,
"let's find the *root* of the problem here."

"It might possibly be hereditary,

a branch of your family tree?"
Triffid wasn't moved at the sarcasm,
as the doctor could plainly see.

"I think this will pass quite soon,
you appear to be deciduous."
"At least when autumn comes
you'll not appear so ridiculous!"

"I'll give you a course of tablets,
so take them three times a day."
"Will it cure the condition?" Triffid said.
"No, but it'll keep the greenfly away!"

ZOMBIELIEVABLE

The cemetery earth erupted
as all the living dead arose,
dragging out their rotting bodies,
spilling soil from ragged clothes.

They staggered from resting-places,
away from their headstone and tomb,
down the hill they trooped together,
silhouetted by a huge, harvest moon.

The mass of corpses surged together
pouring out through the cemetery gate,
strutting on towards a lamp-lit house,
those living there unaware of their fate.

Shattering doors and bursting windows,
as shrill screams of terror rent the air.
A family cowered in the living room,
all terrified, like mice in their lair.

Flesh crumbling arms outstretched,
the chilling stance of a mindless killer.
A zombie lunged to switch the TV on,
in time for Michael Jackson's "THRILLER!"

WEREWOLF – WASWOLF – WHATWOLF?

A full moon painted the woodland
a slick coat of eerie, silver grey.
Something stirred in the undergrowth,
its presence about ten feet away.

I swiftly turned and ran in panic,
my heartbeat began to race.
Dashing into bushes and trees
branches tore and scraped my face.

I gasped frantically for some air
my lungs were about fit to burst,
but close behind me came a howl,
I knew it and feared the worst.

My muscles aching fearfully,
my poor legs seemed to burn,
the fierce growling came closer,
but I didn't even dare to turn.

A thick tree root tripped me,
I crashed down to the floor,
but scrambling to my feet

and turning around, I saw...

There, before me, silhouetted,
in the moonlight's spectral glow,
a pale face, now quite familiar,
smiling wickedly, chuckling low.

As I stood panting and gasping
the figure just laughed out loud.
"You nearly wet yourself there,
you scaredy-cat, big-girl's blouse."

The full moon splashed across
my own brother's smirking face,
but the smirk suddenly vanished
as amazement took its place.

He staggered backwards shocked,
choking on words he could not find,
He turned dashing madly away,
and I followed on closely behind.

He thrashed away panic-stricken
through the bracken and the bush,
his clothing and flesh torn by thorns
undaunted in a headlong rush.

He fell, crumpled and exhausted
into a small clearing by a pool.
The full moon watched within it
gleaming the reflection of a jewel.

A hideous, snarling howl hit the air
and I touched my sweated brow,
I touched only matted hair and growled,
"WHO'S WET HIMSELF NOW
WOOOOOOOOO?"

JEKYLL AND HYDE POTION

Doctor Jekyll clutched at his throat,
his foaming glass dropped to the floor.
His features changed very rapidly,
his light voice whispered to a roar.

His fiery eyes bulged, bloodshot red,
as fangs curved over his bottom lip.
Hair sprouted rapidly across his cheeks,
evil had him clutched in a vice-like grip.

The foulest brew had done its trick,
his form changed from good to bad.
Mr Hyde growled deep within his throat,
"That's the worst cup of tea I've ever
had!"

COUNT CALORIES

A vampire who loved garlic bread,
found he feared spareribs instead.
He went quite weak at the knees
at the sight of hot dog with cheese
and ketchup just made him see red.

Sausages sent him into convulsion,
corned beef gave his bowels propulsion.
With ulcers and raging toothache
from a microwave, veal pasta bake
while pork pies filled him with revulsion.

Bacon caused him to shiver and shake,
a lamb chop made his nerves quake.
But what distressed him for sure,
was the dark curse's only cure,
of impaling his heart with a steak.
(Gammon, of course.)

VAMPIRE SPOTTING

I could tell that the man was strange,
not actually a real human at all.
In the bus shelter, waiting for the 41,
it was just him and me, that's all.

Maybe it was the flashing yellow eyes
that undoubtedly gave him away,
or maybe the long black cloak he wore,
that caused me not to want to stay?

Possibly his pale, sunken cheeks
with that unsettling, sickly grin,
or the long, bony, wrinkled fingers
that scratched at his pointy chin?

It was probably his purple lips
exposing his sharpened teeth,
or maybe the way he just floated,
the ground not meeting his feet.

Whatever it was I found distasteful,
was solved by giving him a push,
'cause not even the Prince of Darkness,
can suck blood from the wheels of a bus!

A CHRISTMAS TALE FROM THE DEVIL'S DISCIPLE

Oh hell, it's Christmas time again,
and the boss is a devil to please.
Come to think of it, he *is* the devil,
and he hates all Christmas trees!

I'll nip up to the shops in my break,
and buy him something really nice.
I can't get much on a disciple's wage,
since it's all such a hell of a price!

Charging through the shopping mall
with my credit card at the ready,
I buy a great present pretty quickly,
I do hope he'll like the pink teddy?

I stop off for a Cornish cream tea
at the quaint, Olde Willow tea-room.
It's quiet after all the demon shoppers
tearing around to meet their doom.

The tea-room doesn't seem to mind
my slightly pungent, sulphur smell,
though the Earl Grey tea and fruit scone,

certainly went down pretty well.

I get back to my work at long last,
making lists of evil people and places.
I add shopping malls to the very top
and shop assistants with sour faces!

I sneak Satan's gift, tied with tinsel,
down inside his stinking, woolly sock.
Too bad he was wearing it at the time,
it gave him quite a yule tide shock.

He screamed abuse at me for the bear,
he says pink teddies are useless slime,
but then I noticed he put it on his pillow
to snuggle up to at beddy-boo time!

JAWS RETURNS

The black tail fin is unmistakable
a great, white shark was abound.
Screams rent the air like thunder,
with a dun-dun-dun-dun sound.

Electrifying panic fuels the soul
with a survival maddening dash.
Don't dare to glance behind you,
you don't want to cause a splash.

You might need a bigger boat
or have to close the beaches,
when you catch sight of its jaws
and how wide its bite reaches!

The scariest of fishes arrives,
bather's blood runs icy-cold,
Here to receive the Nemo award,
ocean's o' fish-al Oscar of gold!

GHOSTS & ALIENS

HAUNTED HOUSEFUL

"BOO," he shouted loud and clear,
enough to frighten the dead,
Mrs Proudfoot wasn't at all pleased
and swiped at Mr Proudfoot's head.

"It was only a joke," he whined,
pretending to rub at his ear.
"You'll be wishing you were dead,"
she said, "if you do it again my dear."

The couple were out viewing at night,
their newly purchased country house,
a creaking old mansion, still occupied,
by something far scarier than a mouse.

Agatha pushed a disapproving finger
through dust an inch-thick on the stair,
a shadow moved on the landing above,
angry Agatha tutted, but wasn't aware.

The spooky staircase loomed upwards,
its banisters so ornate in the gloom,
the night sky flashed with its lightning,
as silhouettes danced in the rooms.

They moved from room to room,
Agatha still muttering all the while,
George shook his head at his wife
her words growing ever more vile.

"A dump of a home you've saddled us
with,
you're a good for nothing worm."
"You even crashed the car on the way,
do you think we've got money to burn?"

"Of course not my dear," said George,
trying to ignore the nagging again,
he also ignored creaking floorboards
and the clanking of a ghostly chain.

Agatha screamed a bloodcurdling yell,
when a cat appeared at her feet.
It arched its back, hissed and spat,
cat and Agatha's heart skipped a beat.

The cat vanished through a cat flap,
moving off like it's tail was on fire.
Agatha cried to George in the kitchen,
her voice getting higher and higher.

"What's wrong now, seen a ghost?"
said George, jokingly waving his arms.
"Ghosts simply do not exist," said Agatha,
wiping the cold sweat from her palms.

"Don't be such an idiot George,
there's absolutely no such thing."
"Next you'll believe in hobgoblins,
and tooth fairies dancing in a ring."

Suddenly came a violent knocking
pounding madly at the front door.
In the doorway stood an Avon lady
who screamed and hit the floor.

"What's wrong with her I wonder?"
Agatha said, with quite a loud snort.
"I think", said George, "our accident,
was much worse than we'd thought!"

The sudden realisation hit Agatha,
she swiped at George once more,
but as her hand passed through his head
she could feel her inner spirit soar.

"Our bodies, they must still be in the
car,"

said George, "we're decidedly dead you see."
"As ghosts we must haunt this house forever,
so Agatha, it's a big old BOO, from me!"

G – G – G - GHOST TRAIN

The car slammed through the doors
the entrance ahead, pitch black.
The doors crashed closed behind us
as we were carried over the track.

A huge skull lit up green before us
as shrill screaming filled the air,
we held each other so tightly,
awaiting the next frenzied scare.

A scarlet axe sliced down before us
as a severed head went flying by,
we rattled round another corner,
something lightly touched my eye.

A witch stirred a cauldron wildly
in a blood red, pulsating light.
In the darkness somewhere above
screeching vampire bats took flight.

Our hands clasped together, aching,
just barely coping with all the fright,
when a giant, luminous, spider,
suddenly swooped down into sight.

The exit doors burst open wide
to bright light and cool fresh air.
Relieved I glanced at my companion,
but found - *there was no one there*!

A SÉANCE IS SUPPOSED TO BE SPOOKY

You know - I can see dead people,
spirits going off to a better place,
but then hanging round after death,
not wanting to leave the human race.

I held a big séance not long ago,
six people sat around a table.
I invoked the spirits to descend
and speak to as many as were able.

To my right sat this very imposing lady,
her height looked down on all things.
Dwarfing two tiny brothers beside her,
who could've been in Lord of the Rings.

On my left were a couple of dainty ladies,
quite prim and proper and thin as can be.
As pale as two pints of semi-skimmed
milk,
in leafy dresses, like silver birch trees.

A sixth sensible person round the table
was a grim man who had only one ear.

He had spectacles that kept on slipping,
so he could only half-see and half hear!

No one appeared and nothing happened,
no weird knocks or voices were heard.
Disappointed I apologised to my visitors,
who began to leave, I felt quite absurd.

I showed them all to the front door
and found six more people there.
I turned back again to my guests,
but they'd vanished into thin air!

The ghosts *had* attended the séance,
no wonder they didn't answer my calls.
I felt an icy ripple gallop through me,
my skin grew goosebumps and crawled.

The six ghosts that all came and went,
made me realise I should be saying.
No spooks should attend a séance,
and just disappear without paying!

TRAVELLING GHOST TO GHOST

Through a solid brick wall of the Old Inn
a figure appeared, a spooky, sickly grey.
The ghost detective switched on his camera
turning the blackest night into lightest day.

The ghost halted and stood quite still
slowly raising up a skeletal hand.
"No publicity please," it screeched,
"but a passport photo would be grand."

"I'm going on vacation soon you see,"
it stated, poking the gap in its hood.
"I tend to go where the spirit takes me,
some say haunting in Scotland is good?"

"You can't leave," the investigator pleaded,
"I haven't managed to prove you exist!"
"Don't worry," said the ghost, departing,
"you're next on the INN-SPECTRE'S list."

MOON MAN

Stepping out from the spacecraft
I faced a hushed, darkened world.
Striding out across the landscape
watching as my planted flag unfurled.

My solo lunar mission setting foot
on the moon's surface had begun.
The Earth glowed brightly above me
like a pale blue, reassuring sun.

All contact with Earth had ceased
I was isolated and totally alone.
I chatted to myself in the silence,
as I was too far away to phone.

The Moon dust lifted each small step,
floating up before settling down.
I moved slowly away from the module
but something odd made me frown.

I gazed back towards my footprints
perfectly formed in the lunar dust.
Beside them a strange set of prints,
my heart leaped out as if to burst.

I quickly turned my helmeted head
from left to right and then behind.
All the emptiness, was truly eerie,
who, or even what, might I find?

Prints were scattered around me,
I stepped backwards truly aghast.
I saw a sweet picture of my Mother
taken on the summer before last.

The prints had fallen from my pocket,
and all were my photos from home.
But picking them up I was handed one,
Good grief, I WAS NOT ALONE!

Falling over backwards I gazed up
at a blue, scaly creature that barked.
Apparently it said my lunar module
had to go, it was illegally parked!

I had to shift it now, immediately
or it would have me towed away.
I dropped my trousers and mooned it,
it squealed and promptly ran away!

It returned with an angry alien crowd
just when I was blasting off away,

it waved a summons with a tentacle,
I'm at Lunar court next Moon-day!

PARKING
TICKET

THE UNTOLD ORIGIN OF PUMPKINS

Pumpkins came from outer space
a couple of million years ago.
Travelling to earth on meteorites,
spitting out seeds to fall like snow.

Sprouting out from the volcanic soil
soon pumpkin forests crossed the land.
Pumpkins swelled out everywhere
even on beaches in nothing but sand.

Fully grown pumpkins sprouted legs
and galloped the plains in packs.
Dinosaurs chased them but failed
as pumpkins left them in their tracks.

Pterodactyls were partial to pumpkins
and flew faster than they could run.
So the pumpkins were soon eaten up,
except for a remarkably clever one.

Now pumpkins used to be bright green
looking like huge peas from the sky.
Pterodactyl's beaks speared them

for their first ever, mushy peas pie.

A clever young pumpkin named Ethan,
painted himself a bright orange coat.
You see orange is invisible to dinosaurs
except for the Jurassic mountain goat.

Painting himself and his family orange
the pumpkins lived secretly for years,
staying well away from the mountains
so none of them had predator fears.

Pumpkins saw the dawn of mankind
and cavemen hunted them for pie.
Man then preferred meat in pastry
and the pumpkins were left to lie.

Years later, they thrived in millions
winning prizes at gardening shows,
until humans then went vegetarian,
and pumpkin pie, was what they chose.

So pumpkins hid from veg lovers
in the supermarket's vegetable aisle,
hated by kids as quite tasteless,
which made all the pumpkins smile.

Until, that is, Halloween arrived
turning pumpkins into lantern lights,
scooping out all their inner mush
and carving out faces for frights.
Pumpkins are wildly popular now,
with no place to hide, they're all sold.
So their masters on Mars aren't happy,
and their invasion plans are on hold.

WE ARE NOT ALONE

All the loneliness and solitude,
the madness of standing still,
the isolation of our ignorance,
the stubbornness of human will.

Our deep, arrogant superiority
sitting lonely on this speck of dust.
New friends are waiting out there,
if we could only learn to trust?

Our stubborn refusal to admit
that mankind is not really alone.
In a great expanse of endless night,
something's hanging on the phone.

Imagination stretched to breaking point,
boundaries still twinkling in the eye.
Tease that thought just a little further,
out to the point where answers lie.

What is never really understood,
is now discounted and dismissed.
Our love of sweet life is cherished
but some just discard it with a fist.

Doubting whether they come in peace
is to show the unknown our fear.
But their appearance may be human,
and they may *already* be here?

Question all of our human existence,
ask just what our friendship is worth?
Ask yourself, is the poet of this piece,
really writing this from planet Earth?

TO BOLDLY GO

We're plotting our way across the stars,
just a careworn passage of dreams,
riddled with reason to hold back time,
in space no one cares if you scream.

An eclipse round the ear of darkest night
throws a cute corona around the moon,
the guiding light points straight to
heaven,
its boundary reached by thought balloon.

A comet's tail paints the heaven's
curtains
with thick brush strokes, deep and wide.
The darkness then swallows its passing
as the endless cosmos allows it to hide.

The earth shrinks away like a pebble
tossed away into a shadowy sea.
A wink of recognition from our shore
then home is gone and so are we.

The far, distant, Dog star beckons.
No, you cannot really be Sirius?

We land and break out a picnic basket,
this vacation is gonna be delirious.

THE TIME-TO-TIME
TRAVELLER

Is this what they all call déjà vu
or have I ever been here before?
I seem to recall
the clock on the wall
said, three fifty-five, not five to four?

The machine flashes coloured lights
like a Christmas tree convention.
This is not the present,
the journey's not pleasant,
I wish I'd not made this invention!

I've been and gone several times
in only a few scant seconds.
As my time re-occurs
it whistles and it whirrs,
Is that H G Wells that beckons?

I return before I even started out,
just how can that possibly be?
I'm sitting over there
in my time travel chair,
and I'm staring right back at me!

I move the setting back again,
everything fades quickly away.
I arrive once more
to a crowded floor,
several 'me's are looking my way!

The room has become quite full,
I hear the echoes of my moans.
From all the 'me's
buzzing like bees,
I feel like I've sent in the clones!

I've given up trying to go back again,
there's no room left to move!
But now a different face
has entered the place,
who sent for that weird Doctor Who?

THE WEIRD & MYSTERIOUS

THE DIPPY-DIPPY SPOON MONSTER

Dippy-dippy spoon monster is sat by your bowl,
it hasn't got a heart, it hasn't even got a soul.
It makes faces in its curves, it sits quietly in wait,
grabbing it's handle, it knows you're too late.

Plunged in cereal, scooping milk and flakes,
into a mouth, wide enough for birthday cakes.
"I'm coming for you," it cries, without any noise,
"I'll get the naughty girls and all the beastly boys."

But there in the darkness, between tongue and teeth
it suddenly gets scared, demanding its release.

"Let me go," it pleads, "it's much too dark
in here."
The spoon monster cries, not
understanding fear.

"I made a big mistake, I promise, I'll be
nice,"
"I won't be nasty, I'll just shovel up your
rice."
So out it goes and scoops again and
again,
hoping you'll stop, but doesn't know
when?

Now in an empty bowl the spoon monster
sits,
its apologies silent, it's nerves are all in
bits.
Soon it forgets and begins plotting once
more,
to scoop you all up in its evil scooping
war.

It will wait quite patiently beside your
knife and fork,
sizing you up, watching you giggle and
squawk.

No need to worry, soon it won't be an
angry spoon,
'cos a dishwasher's dark wash will seal
it's doom.

DEAD END JOB

Twelve-o-clock strikes, the midnight
hour,
amid granite gravestone two men cower.

With spades in hands and lantern nearby
they set to work where dead people lie.

A saucer-eyed owl then hoots his unrest
at finding the two unwelcome guests.
The earth is now broken, a hole appears,
over this soil were shed many tears.

Soon their spades hid the wood below
and the dirt-covered coffin begins to
show.
Wood splinters and cracks, the lid falls
away
all bathed in the flickering lantern's ray.

The features of a corpse could now be
seen,
a grim, crumbling face of a mouldy
green.
William Burke then reached right down,
gripped with thoughts of a golden crown.

But stopped when the death-dealing crook,
spotted the corpse had a blood-red book!
Its eyes popped open, its stare was grim,
its lips parted slowly, dribbling down it's chin.

"It's whispering to us," the grave robber cried,
the other was silent, transfixed, terrified.
"Snap out of it Bill," he shouted at his friend,
as the dead man lifted from an interrupted end.

A gurgle issued of incoherent speech,
Burke stooped as close as he dared reach.
He was close enough to see its eyes glisten,
he even held his breath just so he could listen.

Smelling the foul breath, the corpse then spoke,

cockroaches spilled out distorting it's
croak.
His heartbeat raced, his stark fears were
rife,
he heard the words,
 "WILLIAM BURKE, THIS IS YOUR LIFE."

THE STATUE THAT MOVED

"That statue, did you see it?" the man
exclaimed,
his shrill, excited voice becoming quite
pained.
"It moved, I saw it, just then, didn't
you?"
He said, to the passers-by as they flew.

Wondering whether he should also
mention,
that the eyes had glared, right in his
direction.
"I saw nothing," said a man, moving
swiftly away.
"It moved I tell you, please, believe what
I say."

A lady with a pram frowned at his odd
claim,
muttering, "Poor deluded man, what a
shame."
No one stopped, they all thought him
mad,

well, a statue that moved, it's really quite
sad.

He was totally alone, all about him had
fled,
looking up at the statue, was he off his
head?
Seeing that no one believed his crazy tale
he climbed onto his stand and turned
stony pale.

He whispered, "No one believes we
exist,"
"we're all safe as safe can possibly be."
The other statue simply nodded and
smiled
as they both fell silent beneath the tree.

THE THING

The thing stepped in, I hid from view,
a hideous form, whatever shall I do?
From my vantage point behind the chair
I could see the fiend with its evil stare.

It moved on flimsy covered limbs,
the floorboards creaked each pace.
I couldn't even bear to look upon
its quite truly ghastly, pallid face.

Attack I must and launching forth
I see that this thing does likewise.
It holds back when I hold back,
is it something that I recognise?

I wave a hand, it waves straight back
I'm just now beginning to understand,
why a tongue snakes out as mine extends
and knows everything that I've planned.

It's not quite as ugly as I first thought,
in fact, well, it's good-looking really.
And if I switch on the lamp just now
I can see myself perfectly clearly.

VOODOO YOU DO?

Aimi Doolally plunged big hatpins,
wildly stabbing a lifelike doll.
She muttered magical words,
then hurled it angrily at the wall.

"Why won't it work?" she screamed,
"I've been trying it out for weeks."
"I enrolled at the Witches Night School,
but I've learned nothing from those
freaks."

"I want to get rid of my husband David,
he's a right royal pain in the butt."
"He's a boring wimp, he's a weakling,
with the charisma of a cashew nut."

"A little voodoo hex will see him away,
I'll plunge the fool six feet under!"
"If I can only perfect the magic words
I'll rip his useless guts asunder."

"I've been trying this so very hard
it's all given me a terrible pain."
"It's a searing, burning sensation,

micro-waving my poor little brain."

"My legs are on fire, they're sizzling,
I'm lost, what the hell is going on?"
"David, David help me, you twerp,
my toes are shrivelling - *they've gone*!"

David entered in a long black cloak
wearing a tall, starry, conical hat.
"Yes Aimi dear, you screeched me?
Just how can I help my little bat?"

Aimi saw a strange doll in her likeness,
gripped very tightly in his little fist.
She saw pins protruding out from it,
she couldn't speak, she just hissed.

"The night school I went to." she croaked.
"Yes," said David, "I did it too - *by post*!"
"And I passed the lot with flying colours,
so now, Aimi dearest - you're toast!"

SAMHAINOPHOBIA

I think I've got Samhainophobia?
That's a real fear of Halloween.
I can't stomach those pumpkins,
candle-lit, grinning so mean.

Kids dressing as little monsters,
which figures, scares me to death.
To avoid them I hide in a cupboard,
and even need to hold my breath.

They say that they're after candy,
but I know they're certainly not.
They actually *are* little monsters,
creating some truly wicked plot.

I'll never ever let them snatch me,
dragging me to Halloween-land.
Mummified in a trick-or-treat bag,
the season should really be banned.

Hang on, I think I'm getting better,
it must be some virus-type thing?
I'm binge-watching scary movies,
and keen for the doorbell to ring.

I turned my garden into a graveyard,
black bats hang from my bedroom wall.
I play 'The Monster Mash' full volume,
on my ceiling hairy spiders crawl.

Yes, I've lost the phobia, I'm good now,
I love a pumpkin light's fearful glare.
And since I caught the zombie plague
I don't need a scary costume to wear!

Halloween
not
allowed
here
Trick or Treaters
go
away

HOT PROPERTY

The unpleasant Mr Taylor–Snyde
entered a posh clothing store.
His intent was to steal a new jacket,
to replace the old one he wore.

He tried on several styles until
he found one that fitted just right.
He hung his old jacket in its place,
the old thing was getting too tight.

He boldly made straight for the exit
proudly wearing his stolen swag.
An assistant called out: "STOP THIEF!"
He forgot to remove the price tag.

Down the escalator he sprinted,
his temperature began to rise,
he guessed running made him hot,
'til smoke drifted past his eyes.

Through the revolving doors he ran,
customers and staff hot on his heels,
flames curled out from his pockets,
bursting from his collar and sleeves.

His jacket became a ball of flame,
his head was glowing like a coal,
a girl shouted "STOP, IT'S NOT A JACKET!
"IT'S REALLY A BLAZER YOU STOLE!"

I COULD MURDER A BOWL OF CORNFLAKES

At midnight rice crispies were stabbed
and a box of porridge oats died the same.
A Weetabix gang were all strangled,
and Bran Flakes just went up in flames.

A group of Sugar Puffs were drowned,
and some Cheerio's met the same fate.
All beaten up, crumpled and battered
in a display of milk-curdling hate.

WHODUNNIT, AND WHY,
police forces of the world are baffled,
with this gripping, nail-biting thriller.
They only know one thing for sure,
it's the work of a *cereal* killer!

WHERE DO BAD PEOPLE GO?

Along with millions who passed away
I stand on an escalator going down.
I can't see the beginning of the line
or even the end, so I deeply frown.

The huge line seems to go on forever,
it's an incredibly long, boring queue.
I stand in line as all the backs descend,
watched by mini devils, eating spicy stew.

As the escalator keeps on descending
going down hour after hour after hour,
I suddenly feel I need the loo and
wriggle,
can I hold it in, have I got the power?

I shout out to a little demon attendant,
"Hey you, I need the toilet – *now!*"
He just shrugs his red, spiky shoulders
I think it means I've to wait – but how?

You'd think being dead would stop
the needs of a body now it's gone?

But I'm crossing my legs like mad,
it seems, toilets in hell - they've none!

Oh, wait, I've just realised, this is Hell,
I'm supposed to suffer, now I see.
But it's a cruelty too harsh to stop you
when you're really dying for a pee!

IT MAKES PEOPLE DISAPPEAR

On board the Bermuda cruise ship
a fun cabaret was well under way.
Passengers were dancing to a band,
as night parted company with day.

In the sweltering darkness they partied
the cool jazz band were sizzling hot,
playing on continuously until dawn,
when suddenly they had to stop!

The guys in the band were all panicked,
playing Bermuda was as they'd feared.
They would need another musician now,
the guy on the triangle had disappeared!

THE PAIN IS BACK

A policeman came across a troubled man
as he patrolled along his beat one night.
The man was acting in a strange manner,
apparently battling, with himself, in a
fight!

As the policeman drew near he observed
that the poor man was struggling in vain,
with something attached to his throat,
causing him some considerable pain.

"How can I help?" said the officer noting,
tentacles sprouting from the guy's back.
The man then choked a strangled plea,
and the officer gave it a hefty whack.

The heavy blow his truncheon inflicted
made the tentacles break suddenly free.
"Thanks," said the man, clutching his
spine,
"I've got a bad back that's just killing me.

GIVE ME WINGS

Someday I'm sure I'll do it,
I'm certain that I can fly.
With the aid of some wings
I can accomplish things,
even drunken angels get high.

I want to sail right up there
between the white and blue.
But with this ravaging fear
I'm still quivering here,
watching the boarding crew.

A high, phobic fence exists,
keeping me away from flight.
I don't want to let it beat me,
I should never let it defeat me,
although my demons might.

A far-flung, foreign, sunny clime
is quite well within my reach.
If I don't give in and refuse,
I do have the right to choose,
isn't life such a cruel beach?

That's it, I'm up here in the air,
swallowing sights I've never seen.
Breath-taking, awesome plumes,
sailing in cloud blossom blooms,
no earthly country is this serene.

Wait, although my mind's aloft,
I know my heart's still standing.
The whole world's open wide,
it's inviting me to come inside,
but what's that about us landing?

TIME PIECES

A grandfather clock chimed
midnight
clanging loud and clear in the hall.
As the last chime struck and
echoed,
the clock moved away from the
wall.

It edged its way along the carpet
rocking about from side to side.
It reached the living room door
and then it nudged it open wide.

Lumbering forward into the room,
lined with clocks of every kind,
it seemed to stand in judgement,
attempting to make up its mind?

It turned to a Royal carriage clock,
an antique piece of Kings and
Queens.
The pendulum swung from its
case,
bashing the clock to smithereens.

Turning, it crushed a glass-domed
clock
that exploded right across the
room.
Its long pendulum sliced like a
sword,
scores of clocks soon met their
doom.

An old, oak, wall clock chimed in
protest
trying to stop this insane
slaughter.
The grandfather ignored all the
pleas,
chopping it viciously into quarters.

Grandmother clock ticked him off
asking, why all this destructive
will?
He chimed he was bored in the
hall
and had got plenty of time to kill!

TRICK OR TREATMENT

The group of laughing children
hurried excitedly up the path.
A tooth fairy got to the bell first,
a tiny witch couldn't help but laugh

The giggling band formed a semi-circle
chattering with bags at the ready.
Impatient fingers stabbed the doorbell
but the door remained rock steady.

A light from the curtained front window
showed someone was definitely in.
The sounds from a television echoed,
the doorbell battled against the din.

A junior Dracula kicked the door,
a mini Mummy did likewise as well.
The patience of the trick or treaters,
wore as thin as the button on the bell.

Anger and frustration hit fever pitch
as the children assaulted the door.
Tears began as their voices escalated,
they just couldn't stand it anymore.

The porch light suddenly came on
and the group fell silent as the grave.
An angry, elderly voice grew closer,
the row of masks tried to be brave.

The door swung open to an old man
waving a walking stick in the air.
"Get lost you bunch of devils,
you'll get nothing here, I swear."

A Scream-masked child stepped up
raising an orange trick or treat bag.
"You cheeky little sod," said the old man,
stamping the floor like a wounded stag.

He knocked the bag to the ground
and lifted his stick over his head.
They didn't run away as expected,
but held their ground instead.

He shouted at them – "GET AWAY."
They just stood silent in their place.
Swinging his stick at their heads,
a mask fell off - it hadn't got a face!

Shocked, he pulled at the masks,

ripping away every single one.
They all had blank expressions,
all of their features - had gone!

His face went red, he began to choke,
he gripped at his arm and chest.
Collapsing with one final gasp,
falling face down on a silent breast.

The faceless children gazed down
at the lifeless old man at their feet,
and removing their nylon stocking masks,
all shouted - "TRICK OR TREAT!"

Trick
or
Treat

IT'S ONLY HALLOWEEN

There's nobody hiding in the cupboard,
there's nothing creeping under the bed,
there's no beasties behind the curtain,
just a trick or treat bag inside your head.

Don't worry about any scary monsters,
don't think anyone's about to scream,
don't let the Goosebumps run you over.
Keep repeating - it's only Halloween.

THE DEAD END

OH NO, the end of Halloween, it's not - is it?
Now that you've had your slightly scary visit,
will you see darkness as only the lack of light
or still think it hides creepy things that bite?
I hope you find that Halloween has much more,
so just be brave when going through that door
and descending those steps just try and smile,
as not everything you find is evil and vile.
This poem is dedicated to *that* time of year
and shows you really, there's nothing to fear,
except the fear of having nothing to give,
so support Halloween and let all spooks live!

BIOGRAPHY

Martin Richmond is a retired prison officer, with deep roots in Yorkshire, living in Scotland with his wife Sheila. His published works include, *The Trapdoor to Murder*, a collection of murder short stories and *Beasties and other stories,* a collection of horror stories from DEMAIN's 'Short Sharp Shocks!' series. He has won several movie screenplay competitions from around the world and his feature-length, anthology horror movie script, *Trapdoor to Murder* is now in pre-production. His twitter handle is: @hitchcocked

ADRIAN BALDWIN (COVER ARTIST)

Adrian is a Mancunian now living and working in Wales. Back in the 1990s, he wrote for various TV shows/personalities: Smith & Jones, Clive Anderson, Brian Conley, Paul McKenna, Hale & Pace, Rory Bremner (and a few others). Wooo, get him! Since then, he has written three screenplays—one of which received generous financial backing from the Film Agency for Wales. Then along came the global recession which kicked the UK Film industry in the nuts. What a bummer! Not to be outdone, he turned to novel writing—which had always been his real dream—and, in particular, a genre he feels is often overlooked; a genre he has always been a fan of: Dark Comedy (sometimes referred to as Horror's weird cousin). *Barnacle Brat* (a dark comedy for grown-ups), his first novel won Indie Novel of the Year 2016 award; his second novel *Stanley Mccloud Must Die!* (more dark comedy for grown-ups) published in 2016 and his third: *The Snowman And*

The Scarecrow (another dark comedy for grown-ups) published in 2018. Adrian Baldwin has also written and published a number of dark comedy short stories. He designs book covers too—not just for his own books but for a growing number of publishers. For more information on the award-winning author, check out:

https://adrianbaldwin.info/

DEMAIN PUBLISHING

To keep up to-date on all news DEMAIN (including future submission calls and releases) you can follow us in a number of ways:

BLOG:
www.demainpublishingblog.weebly.com

TWITTER:
@DemainPubUk

FACEBOOK PAGE:
Demain Publishing

INSTAGRAM:
demainpublishing